Marked

Norah McClintock

Orca currents

ORCA BOOK PUBLISHERS

Library and Archives Canada Cataloguing in Publication

McClintock, Norah

Marked / written by Norah McClintock.

(Orca currents)
ISBN 978-1-55143-994-5 (bound)--ISBN 978-1-55143-992-1 (pbk.)

I. Title. II. Series.

PS8575.C62M37 2008   jC813'.54   C2007-907390-5

Summary: When Colin accepts a summer job he doesn't expect to
become a criminal suspect.

First published in the United States, 2008
Library of Congress Control Number: 2007942397

Orca Book Publishers gratefully acknowledges the support for its publishing
programs provided by the following agencies: the Government of Canada
through the Book Publishing Industry Development Program and the
Canada Council for the Arts, and the Province of British Columbia
through the BC Arts Council and the Book Publishing Tax Credit.

Cover design by Teresa Bubela
Cover photography by Getty Images

Orca Book Publishers   Orca Book Publishers
PO Box 5626, Station B   PO Box 468
Victoria, BC Canada   Custer, WA USA
V8R 6S4   98240-0468
www.orcabook.com
Printed and bound in Canada.
Printed on 100% PCW recycled paper.

11 10 09 • 4 3 2

To the boys cleaning up graffiti at Main and Gerrard.

chapter one

It all started when I ran into Dave Marsh, a youth worker who was assigned to me the last time I was in trouble. I kind of got the shakes when I saw him. He is one of those dead-serious guys who can look you in the eye and know that you're hiding something from him. He can also tell what it is you don't want him to know. I saw him coming out of a store down the block, and I immediately turned to walk in the other direction. I wasn't afraid of him or anything.

It's just that, well, I didn't want to talk to him, given how most of our conversations had gone in the past.

I was half-turned around when I heard his booming voice call my name, "Colin Watson."

It was as if he had called out "Freeze!" Because that's what I did. I froze. Then I took a deep breath and turned to face him.

The next thing I knew, he was looking me over like he was a drill sergeant and I was some messed-up grunt recruit. Or maybe he was checking me out for stolen goods. But all I had in my hand was a small bag from an art supply store.

"Are you trying to avoid me, Colin?" he said.

See what I mean? He nailed it just like that.

"No, I just—" I didn't know what to say. I never know what to say when I get surprised like that. Dave used to tell me that this was my saving grace—the fact that I'm not quick on my feet. I'm not a bad liar—it's more like

I can't come up with a lie in the first place. Dave said that meant I wasn't cut out to be a bad guy. Maybe that was supposed to make me feel better. But, mostly, it made me feel like an idiot.

"Still drawing, I see," he said, looking at the bag from the art supply store and at the pencil sticking out of my shirt pocket. He never missed a thing.

"A little sketching, yeah," I said with a shrug. I like to draw. I like it a lot. The past year I'd even had a half-decent art teacher who said nice things about my stuff and gave me lots of tips and pointers. She said I had a good eye. It was the best compliment I'd ever received.

"You got a job lined up for the summer?" Every youth worker I ever met was big on kids having jobs. Jobs teach responsibility. They're a positive way to spend your spare time. They give you money so maybe you won't go out and shoplift like I used to.

"I'm looking," I said. It was sort of true. I *was* looking. But I hadn't put in any applications yet. I didn't want to work at a fast-food joint or be a clerk in some stupid store. I wanted to do something interesting. Preferably something outdoors.

His sharp eyes drilled into me. Here it comes, I thought. He's going to give me a lecture about getting out there with my résumé.

But guess what? He didn't.

"I heard about someone who is hiring kids for the summer. It made me think of you. In fact, I was planning to look up your phone number on Monday when I got into the office so that I could call you and tell you about it."

I was so surprised that I almost fell over. I mean, I hadn't seen this guy in eight or nine months. And it wasn't like we were friends or anything. I was just another screwed-up kid, and it had been his job to straighten me out. But here he was, telling me that he had been thinking of calling me and doing me a favor, when he wasn't being paid to help me anymore.

"It's sort of in your interest area," he said. "It's art-related—although not everyone would agree. A couple of the utility companies have been hiring kids to clean up graffiti on utility poles. It pays minimum wage, but it's an outside job. The thing is—"

Here it comes, I thought. The catch.

"There's minimum supervision involved," he said. "Which means it isn't right for most of the kids I work with."

And this is where he surprised me again—big-time.

"That's why I thought of you, Colin. I've been hearing good things about you."

He had?

"If you want, I can get you the information and even put in a good word for you. You can earn some money and study the urban-art landscape at the same time."

I was so stunned that all I could say was, "Uh, sure."

"Great," he said. "I'll call you on Monday with the details."

Monday morning I woke up to the sound of the phone. It was Dave Marsh. He told me where to take my résumé, who to talk to, even what to say. He said he'd already talked to the man in charge.

"He's expecting your call, Colin," he said. "He's looking for reliable kids, and he's definitely interested in meeting you."

Then he scared me a little.

"As far as I can tell, this job is yours, Colin—unless you do something to mess it up."

chapter two

The man in charge was named Ray Mehivic. He was sitting behind a big metal desk. His office was at the back of what looked like a huge garage in one of those industrial parks that's filled with warehouses and small factories. He was talking on the phone when I arrived, but he waved me in. I stood in front of his desk while he finished his phone call.

"You're Colin, right?" he said, hanging up the phone. "Keeping your act clean these days, I hope."

What?

He laughed.

I didn't.

He grinned. "Relax, kid," he said. "I'm not going to give you a hard time. I'm a big believer in second chances. I know how hard they are to come by. So I try to provide them. I try to help out, you know what I mean? And Dave Marsh thinks you're an okay kid. When he heard I was hiring, he put in a good word for you." He looked me over. "He said you were fourteen."

"I'll be fifteen at the end of the summer," I said.

"Everybody makes mistakes," Ray said, leaning back in his swivel chair. "But people can change, am I right?" He stuck out a beefy hand. "Show me what you've got."

It took me a moment to realize that he wanted to see my résumé. I never thought I would say this, but I was glad we had to write a résumé in careers class at school. I handed it to him. It took him forever to read it.

"You got a bike, something to get around?" he said at last.

I nodded.

"You know what the job is?"

I nodded again, but he explained it to me in detail anyway.

"So," he said when he had finished, "are you interested?"

"Yes, sir."

"Sir," he said, smiling like I'd made a joke. "Okay, Colin. You're on. Be here tomorrow morning, six thirty, to pick up your supplies and get your route."

Six thirty?

"In the morning?" I said.

"Yeah, in the morning," Ray said. "The route you're on, it's a nice neighborhood—lots of doctors and lawyers. Plus a lot of aggressive tagging. We like to get that cleaned up before the residents roll their Beamers out of their garages, you hear what I'm saying?"

I sure did. People who live in big houses don't want to start their day looking at graffiti. I bet graffiti in their neighborhoods made them nervous. It probably made them think of gangs.

"You got a problem with the hours or the job, now's the time to speak up, kid."

I told him I didn't have any problems. I turned to go.

"Hey, kid."

I wheeled around.

Something flashed in my eyes. It was a camera.

"For your ID," Ray said. "If the cops see you and get the wrong idea, they can call me."

Cops? If there was one thing I wanted more than anything else, it was to get through the summer without having anything to do with the cops.

Six AM comes fast when you stay up past midnight playing computer games. If it wasn't for my mom, who has to leave for work at six, I never would have got up. She didn't just hammer on my door. No, she came right on in and shook me awake.

"I left you a lunch. It's in the fridge," she said. She was smiling. She had been thrilled when I told her I had a job. That meant

I wouldn't be pestering her for money all summer. "What time do you think you'll be home?"

My job started at six thirty and went to three, including a half hour for lunch. I was supposed to report back to the garage with my work sheet at the end of the day.

"Probably three thirty," I said.

"I'll call you when I finish my shift," my mom said. "You can tell me how it went."

After she left, I almost rolled over and went back to sleep. But my mom's happy face swam in front of my eyes. My mom had it tough. She had me when she was just seventeen. She and my dad got married, but then my dad got sick. He died when I was eight. My mom worked two jobs for a long time. She cut back to one when I started getting into trouble. She thought if she was home more, that would make a difference. It did. It made me want to stay clear of the apartment as much as possible. The last time I got into trouble, I thought her heart would break. When she came down to the police station, she had the same look on her face as she did the night she woke me up to tell me my dad was gone.

That's when she decided she needed help too. She got some kind of grant, and now, in addition to working, she was studying to be a dental hygienist. She had six months to go. She said things would be better for us once she got a decent job. She was really excited about it. She said as soon as she got established, she'd get art lessons for me if I promised to stay out of trouble. And, I don't know, with her being happy and with the new art teacher telling me I had a good eye, I wanted things to be okay for a change. I didn't want any more trouble. So I sat up and swung my legs over the side of the bed.

I got to the garage right on time. Ray was already there, sitting behind his desk with the phone in one hand, a mug of coffee in another and half a cruller on a paper napkin in front of him. He covered the mouthpiece with one hand and told me to see someone named Stike.

Stike turned out to be a large husky guy in coveralls and work boots. He was checking out the girl-in-a-bikini picture that one of the newspapers ran every day.

"You the new cleanup guy?" he said, looking up from the newspaper like he hoped I'd say no so he could go back to staring at the girl.

I nodded.

He sighed, put down the newspaper and heaved himself off the creaky chair. The concrete floor of the garage seemed to tremble as if Godzilla was marching across it. When he reached the floor-to-ceiling metal shelves on the far side, he started pulling down spray bottles.

"You use this to get the graffiti off the poles," he said, handing me a bottle and a bunch of rags. "Don't monkey around with this stuff," he said. "You fool around and get this in your eyes, you'll need one of those seeing-eye dogs to get around."

He handed me a second spray bottle. "After you get the graffiti off, wait a few minutes until the surface is dry and then spray this on. This makes it easier to get the graffiti off the next time."

"The next time?" I said.

"You don't think taggers are going to give up just because you clean up after them, do you?" he said.

I'd never really thought about it.

"If it's a utility pole or control box, it comes off," Stike said. "I don't care if they're pieces or burners—if they're on electric or phone company property, they're gone. Anything on city or private property, that's someone else's problem. You got that? The utility companies are not paying you to take care of someone else's problem."

"Pieces?" I said.

"The so-called fancy crap they put up," Stike said. "Piece is supposed to be short for masterpiece—talk about hyping your own garbage. Burners are the same thing but bigger and with more detail. But you won't get many of those. The poles and boxes are too small. The crews that do pieces hit walls, garage doors, that kind of surface."

He turned and pulled a clipboard from the wall.

"Here's your route," he said, pulling off some sheets of paper that were stapled together. He handed them to me and waited while I flipped through them before he said, "You recognize those streets?"

"Kind of," I said, although I didn't really.

Stike looked at me the way Dave Marsh used to. He trudged over to another shelf and pulled down a battered city map book.

"You can read maps, right?" he said.

I nodded.

He thrust the book at me.

"Don't lose it," he said. "It's company property. You go to the locations on your work sheet. You clean up whatever you see on utility company property. You check off the location and record the time you were there. At the end of the day, you come back here and turn in your work sheet."

There were a *lot* of locations on the sheets.

"There's graffiti at all these places?" I asked.

Stike gave me a look. "You think the boss is going to pay you by the hour to go out there and hope you find something useful to do?" he said. "Look what it says at the top of this page—work order. That means everywhere you go, you work."

"How do you know there's graffiti at all of these places?"

Stike shook his head. "You haven't heard? The utility companies run a campaign every summer. They set up a hotline. Someone sees graffiti on utility company property, they phone it in. The company promises to get rid of it within forty-eight hours. The idea is that if they wipe it out as fast as it goes up, these knuckleheads will give up and move their act somewhere else."

In other words, make it a problem for someone besides the utility companies and preferably in not-so-nice neighborhoods.

"Do I keep at it until I finish?" I said.

"You keep at it until the end of your shift. Whatever you don't finish goes to the top of tomorrow's work order. At the end of the day, I go out and see what you did. You do a lousy job, you're fired. You do a sloppy job, you're fired. You take too long at each site or do too little work, you're fired. Some locations will need more work than others—that's a given. All Ray asks is you do a good job as efficiently as possible. You got it?"

I had it. I turned to leave.

"Hey, kid," Stike said. "Don't forget your ID."

He handed me a photo ID. I had a stunned look on my face in the picture. The ID was in a plastic holder and had a clip on it so that I could attach it to my belt.

"Just in case," Stike said.

I packed my supplies into the milk crate I'd fastened to the back of my bike the night before and got ready to leave.

"One more thing," Stike called as I mounted up. "Keep your eyes open."

"Huh?" Keep them open for what? What did he mean?

"We had a kid last year who ran into some trouble. Some crew didn't appreciate his cleanup. They waited for him one morning and jumped him. Kid ended up in the hospital." He grinned at me as if he were telling me about some fond memory. "Watch the watchers," he said. "If you think you're attracting some of the wrong attention, you let me know. Crews don't scare Stike."

I had the feeling that not much scared Stike. But the thought of getting jumped by a gang sure scared me. I began to wonder if Dave Marsh had done me a favor after all.

chapter three

I leaned my bike against the boulder that marked the entrance to the neighborhood where I was supposed to work. I couldn't imagine living in a neighborhood like that. The houses were all big—not as big as in the richest part of the city, where the houses cost millions of dollars and all had tennis courts and indoor swimming pools. But they were a lot bigger than the houses in my neighborhood and had yards that were either fenced in or surrounded by hedges.

People who lived here didn't have much to worry about, except taggers who ruined how neat and pretty everything was. It must be nice to live in a neighborhood where that was the worst thing that ever happened.

I looked around to see if anyone was watching me. I kept thinking about the kid who had ended up in hospital. I didn't want that to happen to me. But I didn't see anyone at all. Then I thought about it. Nobody would come after me today, I decided. I hadn't done anything yet. They wouldn't be on the lookout until they saw that someone had erased their tags. It wasn't today I had to worry about—it was tomorrow and the next day and the day after that.

The first job on my list was the utility control box that stood just behind the boulder. It was a big gray box with two flat surfaces that were like blank canvases—at least they must have looked like that once upon a time. Now they were covered with tags. Mostly the tags were boring. Each one was done in one color, either blue or black. There was nothing creative about them.

They were just big squishy initials. I don't know why they even bothered. I mean, what was the big deal? Besides the tags, there were letters and numbers in neon pink between the arms of a big cross.

I stared at the neon pink letters. They were wide and slanted, sort of like the lettering on the tags. But they were different too, not like the rest of the stuff that covered the utility box. I wondered if they were some kind of official markings put there by the utility company.

Stike told me to remove any markings I saw on utility company property. These were markings. They were on utility company property. It seemed simple.

But what if they were official markings, like you see painted on the street sometimes when the city is planning to do some work? And what if I got in trouble for removing them?

On the other hand, what if they were graffiti? And what if I left them there and Stike fired me? My mom was so proud of me for getting this job. I thought about how disappointed she would be if I got fired on my first day.

Time was ticking by.

I had three pages of work to do. Stike was going to inspect not just how well I had done the work but also how much I had done. I had to get moving. But first I had to decide what to do about the neon pink markings.

I pulled my sketchbook out of my pocket and flipped it open to a clean page. I copied the cross and the letters and numbers in it—2N 3W—each number or letter in one of the four spaces made by the cross. If it turned out they were important, I could at least tell Stike what they were. I could even put them back if he wanted me to.

Then I got out my spray bottle and rags and I started to work. It took more applications of the spray and a whole lot more scrubbing than I had expected. I started to worry that I would run out of spray before I got through the first page of work. I waited for a few minutes until the surface dried, and then I sprayed it with the second spray bottle.

I was loading my supplies back into the milk crate when I spotted her.

She was holding three leashes in one hand and two in the other. The leashes were those kind with the big plastic handles that pay out the leash like a tape measure, so her hands were really full. She had light brown, shoulder-length hair with streaks of gold in it. She was wearing a backpack. Even with all those dog leashes in her hands, she had a way of walking, tall and straight, that made me think she was loaded with confidence. Well, why not, if she lived around here? I bet at least half the girls in this neighborhood went to private school. I bet almost all of them would end up in university. So why not stroll down the street like you owned it? Why not have five dogs? Three of them were big—a German shepherd, an Airedale and a chocolate Lab—and probably cost as much to feed as my mom spent on me.

She glanced at me, that's it. Just glanced and then turned her head away again, like she had better things to look at. I wasn't

surprised. I was wearing beat-up jeans and
sneakers.

I swung my bike around, rode off the
traffic island and into the street and headed
in the opposite direction from the girl. I had
a job to do. I couldn't fool around with a
bunch of dogs before going to the tennis
club or the yacht club or whatever she had
planned for the day.

Stike was standing out in front of the garage
when I got back.

"You're late," he said. He didn't sound
happy.

I stared at him. I had heard of people
getting in trouble for being late getting to
work. I had never heard of anyone getting
in trouble for being late leaving work.

"What were you doing?" he said. He
thrust out a mammoth hand. It took me
a few moments before I realized that he
wanted my work sheets.

I took the papers from my pocket,
unfolded them and handed them over.

"*Hmph*," he said after he had flipped

through all three sheets. "You did all this today?"

I nodded. I had finished the jobs on the first two sheets and a few of the jobs on the last sheet. But by then it was almost five o'clock. I started to worry that Stike would be gone by the time I got back to the garage. I worried that that could mean trouble.

Stike shook his head.

"You get paid for eight hours, no matter how much time you put in," he said.

"That's okay."

"It's not okay. Ray don't like it when you cost him money," he said.

"But you just said that I don't get paid more—"

"I'm your supervisor. I have to go out and look at what you did. I've been waiting for you a couple of hours now. Ray's gonna have to pay me overtime for waiting around and then for going out to check on you. You better be worth it, kid. You better have done an A-one job."

He folded up my work sheets and headed for a pickup truck.

"Do you want me to come back tomorrow?" I said.

"We'll see," Stike said. He swung his heavy body in behind the steering wheel. He turned the key in the ignition and started to back up the truck. "I'll let you know."

He was gone before I remembered the neon pink letters and numbers on the utility control box. I should have mentioned them. I should have told him what I'd done. I wondered if he would be mad.

chapter four

My mom opened the apartment door when I was still halfway down the hall.

"I thought I heard the elevator," she said. "I thought it might be you." She looked relieved.

"I'm sorry I'm late," I said. "I should have—"

"There's a man on the phone. He wants to talk to you," she said.

I hurried into the kitchen and picked up the phone.

It was Stike.

"A couple of places, you can still see some of the tags," he said. He sounded gruffer over the phone than he did in person. "One place you checked off looks like you did a sloppy job."

"Is that the place with the skull and crossbones?" I said. "Because whoever threw that up there must have used a different kind of paint. The stuff you gave me didn't work so well and—"

"Relax, kid," he said. "I figured that out." There was a pause, and I started to worry that he was going to say something about the neon pink markings on the utility control box.

But he didn't.

Instead he said, "You gonna waste my time and Ray's money again tomorrow being some kind of brown-noser?"

"No, sir," I said.

I heard a rumble on the other end of the phone, like the beginnings of a cave-in. It took me a moment to realize that it was the sound of Stike laughing.

"See you tomorrow, kid," he said.

The line went dead.

"Who was that?" my mom said.

"My boss."

"Is everything okay?"

I glanced at the phone. I had done a good job—that's what Stike had meant even if he hadn't come right out and said it. I'd done a good job. He wanted me back tomorrow.

"Everything's fine," I said. "What are we having for supper?" Suddenly I was starving.

I stared at the work sheet Stike handed me the next day.

"Isn't that the same utility box I started with yesterday?" I said.

"It's the same utility box you're gonna start with every time someone calls in a complaint," Stike said. "It's right out there in the open. Every doctor, lawyer and stockbroker who lives around there drives by it every day. The taggers know it. You start with that—it should go easier now that you treated the surface—then you move on."

Stike was right. I didn't have to use nearly as much spray or elbow grease to get the marks off the box this time. The whole time I worked on it, I kept an eye out for anyone watching me. I wanted to do a good job, but I didn't want to end up in the hospital on account of it.

I moved to the next item on my list—a utility pole on one of the residential streets. For some reason, this particular pole had attracted a lot of attention. There were maybe five different tags on it, not counting a neon orange one that reminded me of the neon pink tag I'd taken off the utility box the day before. If you ask me, it was done by the same person, only this one wasn't a cross. This one was a triangle, with numbers and letters next to the three sides. On the left side of the triangle was the letter *E*; on the right side, the number nine; and underneath, the letter *N*. It was completely different from the tags and pieces I had removed the day before. It looked kind of official, like the cross on the utility box. I decided to copy it down, just in case. Stike hadn't said anything about the one I'd removed the day before, but maybe that was because the city hadn't noticed that it had been erased. I also wrote down where I found it, just in case. Then I got out my sprays and my rags and set to work.

I had half the pole clean when a cop car rolled up the street. It slowed down as it passed me, and I felt myself freeze up. I had to remind myself that there was no way they were here for me. I hadn't done anything wrong. For once I was the good guy.

I didn't look at the cop car as it rolled by. I concentrated on my work.

But out of the corner of my eye, I saw it come to a stop up the street. A man came down his front walk and pointed to the house next door. Two cops got out of the car. One of them talked to the man. The other one walked up the driveway of the house next door.

I finished cleaning the pole I'd been working on and moved to the next one, which was near the house the man had come out of.

The cop who had been talking to the man went up the driveway of the house next door to speak to his partner.

Pretty soon another cop car arrived, and then a police van with the words *Forensic Identification* on the side.

People started coming out of their houses to see what was going on. I heard the first man say, "I came out to get my paper and I looked over at Neil's house, and I saw that his suv was gone, the new one, the Lexus."

"I thought Neil and Melanie were in France," a woman said.

"They are," the man said, nodding. "That's why I called the police. That suv was there last night. I saw it myself. I—"

He stopped talking when the first two cops came back down the driveway. He went over to them. I guessed he was asking them about what had happened, but I couldn't hear what they were saying. A few minutes later, as I was getting ready to move on again, the man came back.

"Just as I suspected," he said to the other people who lived on the street. "Neil's SUV was stolen."

That caused a buzz.

"But I thought he had one of those new vehicles, you know, with a key that has a computer chip in it. You can't start them unless you have the key."

The man nodded somberly. "They broke into the house," he said. "I told the cops Neil keeps his keys hanging near the phone in the kitchen. You know what the cop told me? There's no key there now. They're going to try to get in touch with Neil and Melanie and see if they can figure out if anything else is missing."

"Poor Melanie," a woman said. "She's been looking forward to this trip all year. This is going to ruin it for her."

Yeah, poor Melanie, I thought. She's off there in France, and someone broke into her house and stole her car that costs more than my mom probably makes in a year, maybe in two years.

I packed my gear into the milk crate

and was just getting on my bike to ride to the next job when a cop came toward me.

"Hey, buddy," he said. "Come here."

I told myself again that this time I was the good guy, that I was doing this neighborhood a favor. But that didn't stop me from feeling sick inside.

I started to push my bike over to the cop. But he said, "Leave the bike where it is." He said it in that bossy way cops have. I don't think a cop has ever talked to me without ordering me around, letting me know who was boss.

I put the kickstand down on my bike and walked toward him. My knees were shaking. My mouth was dry.

"What's your name?" the cop said.

"Colin Watson."

"You live around here?"

"No, sir."

The cop looked hard at me, like he was trying to decide if I was trying to be smart, calling him sir like that, or if I was just a nice kid.

"I saw you over at that utility post," the cop said. "What were you doing?"

"Cleaning up graffiti," I said. I unclipped my ID from my belt and handed it to him. He studied it.

"What time did you arrive here?"

I told him.

"Did you see anyone enter or leave that driveway?"

He pointed to the driveway where all the cops were.

"No, sir."

He wrote down the information from my photo ID, asked me for the name of my supervisor and told me I could go.

I was glad to get away from there.

A couple of hours later, I found a shady spot in a small park and sat down to eat my sandwich and drink my juice box. I pulled out my sketchbook. But instead of sketching what was in front of me, I sketched some graffiti. I even played with turning my initials into a tag. Then I looked at what I had done.

Dave Marsh was wrong. This wasn't art.

It was territory marking, like what dogs did. The markings said, Hey, look at me, I was here. It wasn't even nice to look at. For sure the letters and numbers were stupid. Why did kids—I was betting most of the taggers were kids—get such a charge out of spraying their initials everywhere? What was the big deal?

I scrunched up my empty juice box, tossed it into a garbage can and went back to work.

chapter five

A couple of days later I was studying the utility control box in the middle of that traffic island. It was like the thing was lit up or something, the way it attracted tags. I recognized a couple of them—the same tagger, marking his territory over and over again with his initials, the style as recognizable as handwriting. That made me nervous. If the same taggers kept coming back, then they knew that someone was removing their tags every day. That made me think about the kid who had ended up in the hospital. I looked all around, but I didn't see anyone.

Also on the box that morning were numbers and letters around a neon pink cross. I recognized that writing too. The same person who had put a cross there that first time had put another one there. But I still didn't get it. It wasn't initials, like most of the tags I was removing. It wasn't a piece, either. It was different. I copied it into my sketchbook, just in case. Then I sprayed it and was about to wipe it with a rag when something zipped past me, grazing the backs of my calves.

I spun around.

It was a dog, one of those little ones, a Jack Russell terrier. My mom calls them Jack Russell terrorists because of all the trouble they can cause when you leave them alone. A woman she works with left her Jack Russell puppy alone at home and when she came back at the end of the day, her sofa had been torn to pieces. Those dogs have a lot of energy, my mom said. If you don't tire them out, they'll find some way to tire themselves out. Mostly they find destructive ways.

This little Jack Russell was sure energetic.

It raced past me, trailing a leash, and kept right on going.

Someone yelled, "Buster, stop!"

It was the girl. She was wearing a tank top and tan pants, and her gold-streaked hair was pulled back in a ponytail. She was struggling to hold back the rest of her dogs. The German shepherd and the chocolate Lab were yanking their leashes in the same direction that the Jack Russell had gone. The Airedale was pulling in a different direction. A fourth dog, a pug, was sitting on its butt.

"Buster, come back here!" the girl called. She glanced around, like she was looking for something to tie the dogs to. But there wasn't anything.

I dropped my spray bottle and my rag and took off after the Jack Russell. He was moving so fast that he was practically a blur. But he was trailing that leash, and that worked to my advantage. I ran flat-out, and I dove for the plastic reel at the end of the leash.

Got it.

I held fast.

The leash kept paying out. The Jack Russell darted around a corner.

Then the leash went taut. I had a good grip on the handle, otherwise it would have been jerked out of my hands. I started pulling the leash in, like a fisherman reeling in his catch, until finally the Jack Russell darted back around the corner.

By then the girl and the rest of her dogs had caught up to me.

"Buster," she scolded. "Get over here right now."

Buster looked at her with lively eyes. But after a moment, he trotted back to her.

"Good boy," she said, holding four leashes in one hand so that she could scratch Buster behind the ear.

As soon as I put out my hand to give her Buster's leash, the German shepherd growled at me. His ears stood straight up. He barked and lunged at me.

"Cody! Sit," she said firmly. "Sorry," she said to me. "He's a good dog, but he's a guard dog. He's very protective. He listens to me, though. I helped to train him." She took the leash I was holding. "Thanks," she said in a breezy kind of way, like she wasn't all that grateful. "If I'd had to run after Buster with the rest of these guys, I don't know what would have happened."

"That's sure a lot of dog power," I said. "You must really like dogs."

"Buster is the only one that's mine," she said. "And, really, he's my brother's. I'm looking after him for a while."

"So, the rest of the dogs..."

"I walk them. It's my job."

I guess the surprise showed on my face, because then she said, "What's the matter? You never heard of a dog walker?" Like I was a moron or something.

"Sure," I said. "I just thought–" I shut my mouth. I didn't want to say anything that she might take the wrong way.

"You just thought what?"

"Nothing."

Her eyes were dark brown. They stared right at me.

"What did you think?" she said.

"Well, if you live around here..."

"I don't," she said. "My clients live around here. There's a big difference, believe me."

The way she said it, it sounded like she was glad she wasn't part of the neighborhood. I didn't get it. Who wouldn't want to live in a nice house with expensive cars in the driveway? If you lived around here, for sure your mom wouldn't have to work at some lousy minimum-wage job. For sure the highlight of her life wouldn't be getting a diploma so she could be a dental hygienist.

"Do you mind?" she said. She handed me a couple of leashes—the ones for the Jack Russell and the pug. While I held them, she adjusted the straps of her backpack. She took the leashes back. "I have to go," she said. "I'm on a schedule. I have to deliver these guys home and pick up the second shift. Nice meeting you, I'm sure." And there it was, that half-breezy, half-sarcastic tone that made me wonder what I had done wrong. She was long gone before I realized that we hadn't really met at all. I had no idea what her name was, and I hadn't told her mine. She hadn't even asked. Well, why would she?

I went back to work. I told myself I wasn't going to think about her, not even for one second. Maybe she didn't live around here, but she sure acted the way I bet most of the girls in this neighborhood did, all stuck-up and superior. I told myself that I didn't care if I never saw her again.

But if that were true, why couldn't I get her and her brown eyes out of my mind?

chapter six

By the end of my first week on the job, the thrill was gone—not that there had been much of a thrill to begin with.

"If the utility companies want to get rid of all the graffiti so badly, why don't they just hire someone to watch their property?" I said to Stike one morning while I refilled my spray bottles and packed some fresh rags. "The taggers always go back to the same place."

"*Hmph*," Stike said. He was deep into his newspaper.

"I'm serious," I said.

Stike glanced up at me. He looked annoyed that I was distracting him from catching up on what had happened in the city since the last time he'd read the paper.

"You think the utility companies would be paying your salary if this didn't work?" he said. "Ray has the contract to maintain the utility poles in this area. You're just one of a couple of kids working for him. He had a kid working in Hillmount all last month." Hillmount was a nice neighborhood, almost exactly like the one I was working in. "The taggers got tired of their stuff being removed. They moved on. We haven't had a call from there in two weeks now. We re-assigned the kid to another neighborhood. There are other contractors with other kids cleaning up across the city."

"Yeah, but it looks like it's always the same guys," I said. "At least, it is where I'm working. I recognize their tags. Take the utility control box I'm always starting with. I bet if the utility companies got someone to watch that box for a couple of nights, they could catch the guy easy—"

"Tick-tock," Stike said, holding his watch out to me.

Right.

What did I care what the utility companies did? They were paying me, weren't they? I had a job, didn't I?

Still, I knew I was right. I decided to keep track of the graffiti I removed, so I could prove to Stike that it was always the same guys.

When I got to the utility control box, I copied all the tags I found into my sketchbook before I sprayed them and rubbed them out.

I did the same at the next stop. Besides initials that I recognized, there was another one of those neon orange triangles. This one said *W* to the left, 7 to the right, and *S* underneath. I copied it and cleaned it off along with the rest of the tags on the pole. I was moving down to the end of the street when I passed a house that had a tall hedge all the way around it—so tall that I couldn't see the property until I was riding past the end of the driveway.

An ambulance was parked beside the house. There was a cop car next to it.

A couple of people were standing in the driveway talking to the cops.

One of the cops turned as I rode by. He looked right at me. It was the same cop who had asked if I'd seen anything the day the SUV was stolen. I was shaking all over as I passed him.

My next stop was at the end of the street, practically out of sight of the house where the cops were. I wanted to keep going, to get as far from the house—well, the cops—as possible. I had to tell myself that I had a job to do and that I hadn't done anything wrong.

I stopped where I was supposed to stop. I tried to concentrate on what I was supposed to be doing. But I couldn't keep myself from looking back down the street to the house where the cops were.

Every so often a few neighbors would come and stand on the sidewalk at the end of the driveway. They were probably trying to find out what had happened.

I worked quickly.

Two women in running gear jogged toward the house. They stopped at the end of the driveway and ran in place while they talked to the people who were just standing around. After a few minutes, they started running again. They ran past me and then stopped. One of them jogged in place while the other one bent down to tie her shoelace. The one who was jogging in place said, "If she hadn't gone downstairs to get a glass of water when she did, she never would have heard a thing—she's as deaf as a post. I hope she's going to be okay."

"This area used to be safe," the other one said. She started to re-tie her other shoelace. "But that's the third break-in in a few weeks. Joe's got a call in to a home security company."

"I wish Rob would do that too," the first one said. "He put security stickers on the windows. He thinks that's enough to deter a break-in, but I don't know."

Just like that she turned her head and saw that I was listening to her. She gave me a frosty look, like, how dare I eavesdrop on her. I finished up what I was doing. The two of them started running again.

I was packed up and was getting back on my bike when someone called my name.

It was that same cop.

I stood where I was while he walked down the sidewalk toward me. He wasn't that tall, but he was built. I bet he worked out. I bet if you punched him in the gut, it would feel like punching a brick wall. He had a way of walking that let you know he wasn't afraid. Well, why should he be? He had a gun and one of those batons, plus pepper spray and a radio right there on his right shoulder so that he could call for backup anytime. I had nothing.

"Can you account for your presence here?" he said.

"Yes, sir." I unfolded my work order and held it out to him.

He scanned the pages, looking up at me every couple of seconds to make sure

I didn't try anything. He handed the pages back to me.

"You've been in a few scrapes before, isn't that right?" he said.

He must have checked up on me after the last time he talked to me, so there was no point in denying it.

"Yes."

Across the street, I saw the girl with the dogs. She was heading back toward the house that had been broken into.

The cop asked me some questions about my job.

The girl with the dogs paused for a moment opposite the house that had been broken into. Then she crossed the street and talked to the people who were standing there. They seemed to know her pretty well. I wondered if any of them were clients of hers but decided they weren't because nobody paid any attention to the dogs.

The cop asked me how I knew to come into this neighborhood. I told him that it was all up to the utility companies.

"They have this graffiti hotline," I said. "I guess people around here call in a lot."

The cop didn't say anything except, "You can go."

I got on my bike. I glanced back, looking for the girl. I didn't see her, but there was the cop, staring at me as if he were trying to decide whether to arrest me. I felt like pedaling as fast as I could to get away from there. But that would probably make him suspicious, and I didn't want that. I sure was glad that my next stop was two streets away.

chapter seven

I calmed down a little once I was away
from the cops. I concentrated on what I
was supposed to be doing. I copied down
the graffiti that I found. And after a while,
I started to notice something new. I found
different initials in different places, but no
matter what the initials were, the style was
always the same. Maybe I was wrong—I'm
no expert. But I do have a good eye. And
what my eye was telling me was that a lot
of what I was finding, including the neon

graffiti, looked like it had been done by the same person.

Finally, I took a break for lunch. One good thing about the neighborhood where I was working was that there were little parks everywhere. There must have been six or seven. None of them were big. A couple of them had swings and slides for little kids. One of them had a sandbox with a lot of toys in it. That made me stop and stare. If anyone left toys in a sandbox in my neighborhood, they'd be gone before you knew it. A couple of other parks just had a few benches. In one park, I saw old people feeding the birds. In another one, I saw dog owners letting their dogs fool around.

I chose a quiet park and sat on a bench to eat. While I munched my sandwich, I glanced around. Someone was sitting with her back to me on a bench at the other end of the park. I didn't realize at first who it was. In fact I don't think I would have realized at all if it hadn't been for Buster.

He was off his leash and was frisking around, chasing a squirrel one minute, sniffing the base of a water fountain the next and racing in circles around the bench right after that.

That's when the girl turned. She said, "Buster, sit."

Buster raced around the bench again. He didn't stop until the girl unzipped her backpack and reached inside. Then all of a sudden he plunked his butt down on the ground and watched her, his ears pricked up like little sails.

"Good boy," the girl said. "Lie down."

Buster hesitated.

"Lie down," the girl said again, firmly but patiently.

Buster dropped his front end down onto the grass in front of the bench.

She popped a treat into Buster's mouth.

Buster stayed put.

Then the girl saw me watching her. She turned away like I was poison, even though I had caught Buster for her that time.

I got up, dropped my sandwich bag into a garbage can and walked over to her.

I guess I startled her because she dropped the paper she was holding. I was going to pick it up for her, but she snatched it from the ground first. It looked like a letter. I guessed it was personal.

"Hi," I said.

She just stared at me.

"I saw you this morning talking to those people," I said. "I heard what happened to that woman."

"You *heard*?" she said.

She was acting like she was mad at me for something. But I hadn't done anything.

"I heard someone say her place was broken into. I heard a couple of women talking about getting better security. One of them said her husband just puts up security stickers. He thinks that will protect his house."

"Yeah?" she said, her face still serious. But now she seemed interested in what I was saying. "You mean, those women who were jogging?"

I was surprised that she had noticed me near those women.

"Yeah."

"The blond one said that, right?" she said. "She's out all day, and her husband travels a lot. I asked him if he wanted me to walk his dog for him, but he said no. He'd rather leave it cooped up in the house all day than pay me ten dollars to walk it."

"It wasn't her," I said. "It was the other one—the one with the dark hair."

She looked at me for a moment.

"I saw a cop talking to you," she said finally.

"He saw me working near a house that got robbed last week," I said. "Then he saw me again today. He's probably wondering if it's a coincidence."

She stared at me with those dark brown eyes. "And you told him it was, huh?" she said.

What kind of question was that?

"Yeah," I said. "Of course." I glanced at the paper in her hand. "So, who is that from? Your boyfriend?"

"My brother."

"Your brother who owns Buster?" I said.

She nodded.

"Where is he? On vacation somewhere?"

She gave me a sharp look. I felt as if I'd said something wrong, but I couldn't figure out what. She stood up and snapped a leash onto Buster's collar.

"My name is Colin," I said.

She didn't tell me her name. Instead she just turned and walked away. Well, big surprise. For all I knew, she had a boyfriend—maybe he lived in this neighborhood.

chapter eight

It was a week before I saw the girl again, and then I saw her twice in one day.

The first time was in the morning. I was cleaning a utility pole when I spotted her on the other side of the street with her five dogs. She didn't look at me. But I looked at her. Maybe she wasn't friendly, but she sure was pretty.

A car stopped beside her. The driver rolled down his window and said, "Alyssa! I thought that was you."

Her face lit up, and she looked even prettier. Alyssa was the perfect name for her. It seemed to go with her gold-streaked hair.

"Dr. Evans," she said. "Hi."

"Mrs. Petroff was in the clinic the other day. She asked about you. She's thinking of getting another dog and wanted to know if you were still in the dog-walking business. She said she hadn't seen you around for a while. I'll have to tell her you've moved your business to another neighborhood."

"Thanks to Mrs. Linzer," Alyssa said. "She hired me to walk Freddie." I wondered which one was Freddie. "She gave my name to some of her neighbors. But I'd go back to Hillmount if she needed me, especially to walk a puppy."

"I'll tell her," Dr. Evans said. "And I could use you back at the clinic on Saturdays once summer is over, if you're interested."

"That would be great," Alyssa said.

"You have a way with animals," Dr. Evans said. "We've missed you. You have a good summer, and I'll see you in September."

He rolled up his window and drove away.

Alyssa glanced across the street. She saw me, but she didn't wave or smile—not that I expected her to.

I saw her again later that day. This time it was nowhere near the neighborhood where we both worked. I was on my way home after handing in my work sheets to Stike. My mom had class that night. I knew she had left me something I could warm up for supper, but now that I was making money, I decided to get myself a meatball sandwich. I was on my way back to my bike with it when this little white blur with black-and-tan markings hurtled toward me, trailing a leash.

Buster.

He jumped at the bag that had my sandwich in it. I held it above my head. No way was I going to let him grab my supper. I looked around for Alyssa. She was dropping something into a mailbox down at the corner. Buster was yapping and jumping as if he thought he could leap right over my head and snatch my sandwich if he just tried hard enough. Alyssa didn't even notice that he was gone.

I kept the sandwich out of Buster's reach as I scooped up the end of his leash.

"Come on, Buster," I said.

I led him over to Alyssa.

"You lose something?" I said.

When she turned around, I saw that she had been crying. She looked at the leash in my hand and at Buster, who was still yapping and jumping for my sandwich.

"Thank you," she said. She took the leash from me.

"Are you okay?" I said.

Stupid question. Her eyes were all watery. Her cheeks were wet. Her lips were trembling. I could see she was trying hard not to cry in front of me.

She stared at me for a moment. Then she said, "I just heard. My brother is in the hospital."

"Is he okay?"

"He was beaten up." Her eyes burned into me.

"That's terrible," I said. "What happened? Does he know the guys who did it?"

Her eyes went from burning to freezing.

"He was trying to protect me," she said.

That confused me.

"I thought you said he was out of town," I said. I wondered how he could protect her when he wasn't even around.

"Right," she said. "You have no idea what I'm talking about."

The way she said it, it sounded like she didn't believe me. What was going on? Why did she always act like she thought I was lying to her?

"Come on, Buster," she said. She wheeled away from me. I watched her march down the street, moving so fast that Buster's little legs were a blur trying to keep up with her. It was only when I was back on my bike heading home with my sandwich that another question occurred to me: What was her brother trying to protect her from?

I kept an eye out for Alyssa the next day and the day after that. But I didn't see her.

So I concentrated on my work and what I thought was a good plan—convincing Stike that if the company could catch the person doing all the graffiti, they could save a lot of money. My mom laughed when I told her about it.

"If they catch whoever is doing it, you won't have a job," she said.

I told her about the kid who used to work in Hillmount.

"They'd send me to someplace else," I said. "And anyway, if it was nice graffiti, if it was done by someone who really knew how to draw, I wouldn't care so much," I said. "But this is ugly—just stupid initials by someone who's probably trying to make people think there's a gang involved. But there isn't. I know there isn't."

I turned out to be wrong about that.

For a while things were going along so smoothly that I started to think my biggest problem for the rest of the summer was going to be how not to die of boredom.

Then it happened.

I was cleaning a utility pole on a street I had never been on before. I had just removed another one of those stupid triangle markings when a cop car zipped by me. It didn't have its lights or siren on, but it was moving fast. It pulled up to the curb halfway up the block.

A woman came out of the house where the cops had parked. She hurried toward them, and they all stood there for a while. The cops had their notebooks out, so I guess the woman was making some kind of report. She kept waving her arms around, and I could hear her voice from where I was standing even if I couldn't make out what she was saying. She sounded upset.

Then she looked out into the street. She looked right at me. She must have said something to the cops, because they turned too. The woman started down her driveway away from the cops. At first she was walking fast. Then she began to jog in my direction. I turned and looked all around, trying to figure out what had caught her attention. When I turned back again, she was right in my face.

"It was you, wasn't it?" she said.

"*What?*" What was she talking about?

Then the cops were there too. One of them was the cop who had talked to me twice already.

"That boy was hanging around outside Mrs. Eakins' house just after it was broken into," she said.

That's when I recognized her. She was one of the two women who had been out running that day.

"He heard me," she said to the cops. "It's my own fault. Rob is always telling me I should be careful what I say. I tease him about being paranoid, but it looks like he's right."

The cops looked as confused as I was. One of them said, "M'am, if you could just–"

"He heard me," the woman said. Her voice was loud and shrieking. "He heard me tell my friend."

"What did you tell your friend?" one of the cops asked. The other one, the one who had talked to me before, kept his eyes on me.

"I told her that my husband put up security stickers to scare off burglars, but we didn't really have any security alarms. He heard me. He was hanging around and he heard me." She turned to me. "Who did you tell? Who was in on it with you? Where's my car?"

What?

The cop who had spoken to me before said, "I think we should have a talk, Colin." He led me away from the woman. She kept coming after me, but the other cop finally got her turned around. He took her back to her house. The first cop took me over to the police car. He started to explain that he wanted to ask me some questions, but that I didn't have to talk to him if I didn't want to. He said I could phone my mom if I wanted to. He kept asking me if I understood what he was saying.

chapter nine

I felt terrible calling my mom and making her to leave work to come to the police station. She asked me what had happened. She sounded worried, not mad, when I told her. She didn't yell at me. That made me feel a little better.

"I didn't do anything," I told the cops.

"Did you hear Mrs. Franklin say that there was no real security at her house?"

"Yes," I said. "But I didn't know until today where she lived."

I couldn't tell if the cops believed that.

"Do you belong to a gang, Colin?"

"No, he does not," my mom said. She was angry—at the cops.

"Have you ever been a member of a gang, Colin?"

"No," I said.

They asked me a million more questions. I told them how I had got the job. I gave them Dave Marsh's name and Ray's and Stike's. I let them look at my work sheet so that they could see that I had been near that woman's house this morning because I was supposed to be there. They made my mom and me wait while they left the room. When they finally came back, they said, "You can go for now, Colin."

For now?

"He didn't do anything," my mom said. "He's a good boy."

The cops didn't reply, but one of them held the door for my mom.

Stike wasn't the only person in the warehouse when I got there the next morning. Ray was there too, his arms folded across his chest.

He watched me ride up the long driveway to the warehouse. His eyes never left me. He made me so nervous that my bike wobbled when I got off it. Stike waved me over. He stepped aside to let Ray do the talking.

"The cops called me," Ray said. "They asked a lot of questions about you. What's going on, Colin?"

"I didn't do anything wrong," I said.

Ray looked long and hard at me.

"Do you remember what I said about second chances?" he said finally.

I nodded.

"Well, I meant it. I'm going to believe you, Colin. But if the cops call me about you again, I'm going to have to let you go. I'll have no choice. The utility companies won't like it if the cops think that someone who's working for them is up to no good."

"But I'm not—"

"Keep your nose clean, kid," Ray said gruffly. He turned and went back inside.

"I didn't do anything," I mumbled to Stike.

"Do your job and you'll be all right," Stike said.

It's a good thing I didn't see any cops that day because I sure looked suspicious. The whole time I was working, I looked around to see if there were any cop cars sliding by. There weren't, but that didn't help me relax. Every time I pedaled around a corner, I held my breath. What if my next stop was right near another crime scene? What then?

The same thought was still on my mind when I took my break for lunch.

The cops had questioned me about those break-ins.

That one cop had asked me, "Am I supposed to believe it's a coincidence that every time there's a break-in in this neighborhood, there you are?"

The question had scared me.

Then I thought, it's also insulting to be asked that. I mean, how stupid would I have to be, to be standing right near the scene of the crime every single time? It was bad enough that the cops thought I was a criminal. It was even worse that they thought I was a stupid criminal.

My mom was waiting for me when I got home. I held my breath again. Had the cops called her? Had they been to the apartment?

But no.

"We're going out to eat," she said, grinning.

I stared at her. We were on what my mom called a tight budget. We only ever ate out on my birthday—and that was more than a month away.

"Aren't you going to ask why we're going out?" my mom said. Before I could answer, she told me. "I was offered a job today. As a dental hygienist. I have to pass my exams, of course. But one of the dentists who teaches us has his own practice. He said I'm the best student he's ever taught. His hygienist is moving in a couple of months and he has to find a replacement. He asked me if I would be interested. He said if I do as well as he thinks I will on my exams, the job is mine."

"You'll do great, Mom," I said. "I know you will." No one worked harder than my mom.

When we got home from dinner, my mom went to bed. So did I. We both had to get up early. But I couldn't sleep.

I pulled out my sketchbook and started to flip through it, looking for a blank page. I started to sketch a girl—Alyssa. But it wasn't very good, so I erased it. I stared across my tiny room. I had a whole shelf of books. My mom was a big believer in reading. Okay, so most of my books were secondhand. A whole pile of them had been bought at library book sales for twenty-five cents each. A lot of them were either picture books or books with a lot of pictures in them, like a book about the history of railroads and another full of pictures of animals. My mom bought them so that I could practice drawing. One was about dogs. I flipped through it until I found a picture of a Jack Russell terrier. I propped the book open to that page and started to sketch. I drew it so that the dog was jumping up the way

Buster had jumped up on me. I sketched in his trailing leash. And I drew the same black-and-tan markings that Buster had. It looked pretty good, if you ask me.

When I finished, I flipped back through my sketchbook. I had pages of tags that I had copied. I knew I was right about them. They were done by the same person. But I didn't care about that anymore. All I cared about was keeping my job and not ruining my mom's summer.

The next morning, I got the jitters all over again.

My first stop after the utility control box was on the same street where the first robbery had happened. In fact, it was the exact same utility post.

I was getting my spray bottles out to clean it when I heard a car slow down behind me. One thought flashed in my mind: Cops.

"Hey, kid," a voice said.

I was sweating as I turned around.

But it wasn't cops. It was a man in a regular car.

"Is this Woodside Crescent?" he said.

I nodded.

"Jeez, would it kill them to put in a street sign?" the man said.

I turned and pointed to a sign that was half hidden by the leaves of an elm tree. The man just shook his head.

"Hide it, why don't they?" he said. "Same with the house numbers around here. Would it kill these people to put them where a person on the street could actually see them?" He shook his head again. "I don't suppose you know where number one-two-four is?"

I glanced at the closest house. It was number one-zero-five, which meant that one-zero-six was right across the street.

"Sure," I said. "It's on the north side of the street, nine houses down," I said, counting them off in my head as I scanned the street. "Right there," I said, pointing at the house. Wouldn't you know it? It was the same house that had been broken into my second day on the job.

The man thanked me and drove away. I watched him turn into the driveway.

I finished up and went to my next stop. I didn't think about him or the house until I was sitting in the park a few hours later, eating my lunch.

chapter ten

Alyssa was there, with all five dogs. Cody, the German shepherd, was nosing into her backpack looking for treats. She scolded him and pushed him away. So far she hadn't noticed me. I decided to find someplace else to eat. Then I thought, why should *I* leave? I hadn't done anything.

I sat on the bench farthest away from her, with my back to her. I took out my sketchbook and a pencil, and I sketched the houses across the street while I ate.

Something jumped up onto the bench beside me and lunged at my sandwich.

Buster, trailing his leash again.

Then I heard barking—a lot of it.

I turned. Alyssa was standing there, straining to keep a grip on four leashes while she bent down to grab the leash Buster was trailing. I ducked down and retrieved it for her. She didn't say a word when I handed it to her.

"You're welcome," I said sarcastically.

Her cheeks turned pink.

Buster leaped up onto the bench again. This time he got hold of my sandwich. I was so surprised that I dropped my sketchbook.

"Buster!" Alyssa said. But he had already gobbled up what was left of my lunch. Alyssa picked up my sketchbook and started to hand it to me. Suddenly she smiled. "This looks like Buster," she said, looking at the picture I had drawn the night before.

"It is."

"Did you draw it?"

I nodded.

"It's really good," she said.

"Thanks."

She handed the sketchbook to me. But she didn't walk away. Instead she stood there, looking at me.

"You could be an artist or something if you wanted to," she said.

It was my turn to get red in the face.

"My art teacher said I might want to think about art school," I said.

She frowned. "So why are you doing this?"

"What do you mean?"

"Cleaning off all those marks. Why are you doing it?"

She sure asked strange questions.

"It's a job," I said. "For the summer. The utility companies are only paying minimum wage, but it's better than nothing."

She shook her head impatiently. "What I mean is, why take chances?"

Take chances? Then I remembered what Stike had told me about the kid who got beaten up.

"Did you see something?" I said, trying

not to look as nervous as I felt. "Do you think the guys who did the graffiti are going to beat me up for erasing it?"

She looked at me like she thought I was crazy.

"What are you talking about?" she said.

"What are *you* talking about?"

We stared at each other for a moment. Then she seemed to relax a little.

"I'm Alyssa," she said.

"I know. I heard that doctor say your name—Dr. Evans. What kind of doctor is he, anyway?"

"He's a vet," she said. "I worked for him on the weekends during the school year last year."

"That's how you got into the dog-walking business, right?" I said. "You walk dogs for people who visit that vet." I figured that out from what she had said to him.

She looked surprised, but she nodded.

"Is your brother okay?" I said.

Her eyes clouded. "He's still in the hospital."

"I'm sorry."

She gathered up all the leashes. "I have to go," she said. "I have to get these guys home."

"I should get back to work." I started to get up. "See you," I said, like that was ever going to happen.

"Yeah," she said, smiling just a little, but smiling all the same. "See you."

I watched her go. I wished I was good enough to draw a picture of her from memory.

After she left, I put my sandwich wrapper in the garbage and picked up my sketchbook to put it away. I flipped it open to look at the picture of Buster. Alyssa was right. It *was* good. I thumbed through some more pages. Some of my other sketches were good too.

Then I saw some of the graffiti I had copied—the loopy initials and the other stuff.

I stopped at one page and stared. It was the first triangle I'd cleaned up—the one with the *E* and the nine and the *N*. It was from the street where the first break-in happened. I stared and stared at it.

Then I flipped to the next page where I'd copied another triangle. I stared at that too.

I jumped on my bike and raced back to the most recent crime scene.

I stared at the last triangle I had copied down and counted the houses on the street. My mouth was hanging open. What were the chances? I thought.

Then I saw someone come out of the house. It was the woman who had accused me of being involved in the break-in. I got on my bike and got out of there, fast. I headed back to the park where I'd had lunch so that I could think.

I sat on the same bench and flipped through my sketchbook. I looked at all three triangles.

"Hey," someone said behind me.

I turned. It was Alyssa. She had only two dogs with her now—Buster and Cody, the German shepherd.

"Hey," I said.

"I thought you said you were going back to work."

"I thought you said you were taking the dogs home."

"I am," she said. "I have one to go." She looked down at my sketchbook. Her smile faded. "What are you doing?" she said.

I had been sitting there wondering who to tell. The cops? Would they believe me or would they think I'd been involved? Ray? What would he think? I knew my mom would listen to me. She would believe me. But what about a regular person? What would a regular person think?

"You know the areas where I've been working?" I said. "There's been a bunch of break-ins—at the house where the people were on vacation, at the house of an old lady who's practically deaf, and at a third house that has security company stickers but doesn't really have an alarm system." I had been thinking about it and thinking about it. "I think that whoever broke into those houses knew what they were doing."

"What do you mean?" Alyssa said.

"I think they knew that family was away. And that the old lady was deaf—if she hadn't got up to get a glass of water, she would never have been hurt—"

"What are you saying, Colin?"

"I think someone marked those houses," I said.

"Marked them?"

"Maybe someone who knows the people who live around there left marks to tip off the thieves."

She shrugged out of her backpack and sank down onto the bench beside me. "What are you talking about?"

I flipped to the first triangle and showed it to her. She frowned.

"This was on a utility pole near the first house that was robbed," I said. "It was right in front of number one-zero-five."

She was still staring at the triangle. I could tell she didn't get it.

"And one-zero-five is on the south side of the street," I said. "The house that was robbed was on the north side of the street, exactly nine houses east of where this triangle was."

She still didn't get it.

"It's a code," I said. "*N* for the north side of the street, *E* for the house being east of where the triangle was, nine for the number of houses away." I flipped to the next triangle and explained that one to her. Then the next one. "You get it?" I said. "Whoever painted these triangles onto those poles was tipping off the thieves."

She looked serious as she nodded.

"What are you going to do?" she said.

"Go to the cops, I guess," I said.

It sounded like a good idea until she said, "Are you sure you want to get involved?"

chapter eleven

I stared at her.

"Why wouldn't I want to get involved?"

Cody, the German shepherd was nosing around her backpack again. But he was behind Alyssa, so she didn't notice.

"You don't know who the thieves are," she said. "They break into people's houses. They're probably dangerous."

I gulped.

"Maybe. But the cops are suspicious of me," I said. I had already told her about the cops talking to me after the first two robberies. Now I told her about the woman who had accused me of being involved. "She said I'd overheard what she said about her house having no alarm system," I said. "The cops took me in for questioning. If there's another robbery, and I just happen to be there, they're going to arrest me. I just know it."

Cody grabbed one of the straps of her backpack and started shaking it.

"Hey!" I said.

She turned to see what was going on. The German shepherd must have thought there were treats in the backpack, because he was shaking it hard. The pack opened up and stuff went flying out—her wallet, a hairbrush, a small ball, probably for playing with Buster. A spray can.

Alyssa and I stood up at the exact same time.

We bent down at the same time.

We both reached for the spray can.

I picked it up.

I stared at it.

It was a can of neon orange spray paint.

I looked at it, and then I looked at her.

She spent a lot of time in the neighborhood where the robberies were happening.

She talked to a lot of people in the neighborhood. I bet she noticed things too.

"You knew that house didn't have a real security system," I said. "You knew because I told you."

She picked up her backpack and put her wallet, her hairbrush and the ball into it. Then she reached for the can of spray paint.

"It's you," I said. "You've been leaving those codes, haven't you? You're a thief." She used to walk dogs over in Hillmount too. The graffiti had stopped there—no wonder. She was here now. I wondered how many robberies there had been in Hillmount.

I stared at her. She was so pretty, and she seemed nice. She didn't look at all like a thief.

She was calm. She took the spray can from my hand, tucked it into her backpack and pulled the drawstring to close her pack.

"I don't know what you're talking about," she said.

"Yes, you do. But I don't get it," I said. "You have a job with that vet. You walk all those dogs. Why are you stealing?"

Her eyes flashed. Boy, did she look mad.

"I'm not," she said.

"Right. Let's see what the cops say."

"I'm *not* stealing," she said.

"You're telling them which houses to break into. It's the same thing."

"No, it isn't," she said. "It isn't the same thing at all."

I couldn't believe it. She had just as good as admitted that she was involved. Maybe she wasn't breaking into those houses, but she was working with the thieves. She was telling them where to go.

I backed away from her.

"I'm going to the cops," I said. "You

can come with me or not, it's your choice. But I'm going to tell them what's going on."

She snapped her fingers.

The German shepherd went still. His ears stood straight up. His tail didn't move. He growled at me. She had told me that Cody was a guard dog. Was he also an attack dog?

"If you go to the cops, I'll tell them you were in on it with me," she said.

"You know that's not true."

"I know it now," she said. "But you said it yourself. The cops already suspect you. That woman knows you overheard her. I'll tell the cops you told me what you heard. And you're always there, first thing, getting rid of the marks, getting rid of the evidence. If that doesn't make it look like you're involved, I don't know what does."

I couldn't believe what was happening. She could make big trouble for me. I reminded myself—*again*—that I hadn't done anything wrong.

I turned to leave.

I heard her fingers snap again. Cody growled at me. Then he lunged in front of me, blocking my way.

"I don't want to mess you up," she said. "But I'm not kidding. If you go to the cops, I'll make sure you end up in trouble too. That's a promise."

I turned slowly.

"Why are you doing this?" I said.

She bit her lip. Finally she said, "It's my brother."

chapter twelve

"Your brother is a thief?" I said.

Her eyes flashed again. I think she wanted to punch me, even though she was a girl and I was a lot bigger than her.

"My brother made a mistake, that's all," she said. "He did something stupid—he trusted the wrong person. Now he's in prison."

"I thought he was in the hospital."

"He's in a prison hospital," she said, her voice bitter. "My brother isn't tough. He isn't bad. He's gentle. He wanted to be a social worker, only now he's in prison. It's awful in there, especially if you're like my brother. There are guys in there that bully you. They won't leave you alone unless you pay them—and my brother doesn't have any money."

"Is that what this is all about?" I said. "You're stealing stuff so that your brother won't get bullied?"

"*I'm* not stealing anything," she said again.

"But you're helping them."

"I wanted to stop. I told my brother I wasn't going to do it anymore. That's when they beat him up."

Oh.

"Is that why he's in the hospital?"

She nodded. "If I go to the cops, they'll hurt him."

"If you go to the cops and tell them what's going on, they'll protect him."

She was shaking her head before I finished talking.

"They'll blame my brother. They'll say he's the one behind it."

"But you just said—"

"You don't get it," she said. "He's the one who told me what to do."

"Your brother?"

"I only ever spoke to him. He told me what they wanted me to do. He said if I went to the cops, they would say he was calling the shots. He'll never get out of prison."

"So you find places and you leave those marks to tell them which house."

She nodded.

"But there are so many streets," I said. "What do they do, drive around the neighborhood looking for marks?"

"I leave a sign somewhere else, to tell them which street," she said.

"Where?"

"There's this box," she said. She didn't need to say any more. I knew which box she was talking about—the utility control box. "I leave a sign there, and the next day I leave another one on whatever street it is, to tell them which house. I do a lot of other tags too, you know, so it looks like there are a lot of kids tagging."

"And I'm always there first thing after the robbery, cleaning up the evidence," I said.

"I call this graffiti hotline," she said.

"Yeah, well, lucky for them that your marks are always first on my job list," I said.

She gave me a look. "You think *that's* a coincidence?"

What did she mean by that?

Oh.

"If they even suspect I talked to the cops, they'll say my brother is the ringleader," she said. "And he won't give anyone up—no way. They'd kill him. There's no way out."

I didn't know what to say. But I did know that what she was doing was wrong.

I took a step backward.

The German shepherd growled at me.

I looked at Alyssa. Was she going to snap her fingers? Or did she have a different signal to get Cody to attack?

chapter thirteen

She raised her hand.

What would happen if I ran?

I looked at the big German shepherd. Then I turned to Alyssa.

"It's all a mistake," she said. "My brother never should have gotten arrested. He was just helping a guy he knew move some stuff. It turned out that the stuff was stolen. My brother didn't know. Then the guy—his so-called friend—blamed my brother when he got caught, so he told the cops my brother was in on it. Then, once he was in prison, some other guys started giving him a hard time. I don't want anything bad to happen to him. I want him to get out in one piece."

I believed her. If I had a brother and he was in a jam like that, I'd want to help him. But that didn't make what she was doing right.

"You said it yourself, Alyssa," I said. "These guys are dangerous. They break into people's houses. They beat up your brother. You have to go to the cops."

She shook her head. "No way."

I glanced at Cody again. He still looked like he was ready to attack me. My mind raced. How was I going to get out of this?

Two little kids ran past us on their way to the swings and slides. Two more little kids chased after them. A couple of women pushing strollers followed them. Alyssa looked at them. She called Buster, picked up his leash, and then she stood there for a moment, both leashes in her hand.

"I meant what I said, Colin," she said. "If you tell, you'll be sorry. He's my brother. What choice do I have?"

She turned and walked out of the park.

I didn't know what to do. What if Alyssa told the guys she was helping that I had figured out what they were doing? What if they came looking for me? What if they beat *me* up?

I thought of telling my mom what had happened, but she would just make me go to the police and tell them about Alyssa. What if Alyssa carried out her threat? What if she told them that I was in on it?

Then I had another idea.

Dave Marsh was surprised when I turned up at his office.

"How's the job going, Colin?" he said. "Is everything okay?"

"Not exactly," I said.

I took a deep breath and told him all about the markings on the utility control box and the utility poles. I showed him my sketchbook. I told him about the graffiti hotline and how the first jobs on my work sheet were always the places that had the special markings on them. I didn't tell him Alyssa's name. Not at first. But I did tell him that the person who was marking the houses had been forced into it and that the person was scared.

Dave Marsh leaned back in his chair. His face was more serious than I had ever seen it. I couldn't tell whether he believed me or not. Finally he said, "You want to help this person, is that it, Colin?"

I nodded.

"I have an idea," I said. "But I don't know if it's any good."

He didn't interrupt me while I explained. When I had finished, he said, "I think it's worth a try."

I was so nervous that I thought I was going to throw up. I was sure the cops wouldn't believe me. I think it helped that Dave Marsh was there with me. The cops listened carefully to what I said.

Finally they said, "What about the girl? Do you think she will go along with it?"

That was the biggest problem. I didn't know what Alyssa would do.

"She's just trying to help her brother," I said.

I didn't find out what happened until after it was over. The way I heard it later, one night Alyssa put a neon pink code on the utility control box to tell the thieves which street to go to next. Right after that, she did what she always did—she called the graffiti hotline. The next morning, that box was the first stop on my work sheet. I cleaned the marks off.

The night after that, Alyssa made neon orange markings on a utility pole to tell the thieves which house to go to.

But when the thieves turned up, they got a big surprise.

The police were waiting for them. They arrested them.

They arrested Ray too. Alyssa had been right about that. It was no coincidence that her markings were always first on my work order. Ray was in on it.

They also arrested Alyssa.

It made the news: *Police crack car-theft and burglary ring.* All of the news stories said that the police had been tipped off by a youth who was employed for the summer cleaning up graffiti. One newspaper quoted one of the arresting officers as saying that the ring wouldn't have been broken "if it wasn't for the sharp-eyed young man who figured out what was going on."

"You did a good thing," my mom told me. We were on the way to the police station together. The police wanted to ask me a few more questions.

Alyssa was there too. She was leaving as I was going in. She looked at me, but she didn't say anything.

I saw her again when I came out of the police station. She was standing on the other side of the street.

"I'll meet you at home," I said to my mom. I crossed the street.

"I was really mad at you when the cops showed up at my house, Colin," Alyssa said.

"I thought you ratted me out. Then the cops told me that they knew why I had done it. They said someone told them all about my brother. That was you, wasn't it?"

I nodded.

"They said if I helped them catch the guys, they would see what they could do to help me and my brother. After they arrested the thieves, they came and arrested me. They put handcuffs on me, Colin. And they made me walk past the thieves so that they could see that I'd been arrested too."

"Were you scared?" I said.

"What do you think? But the cops kept their promise. My brother has been transferred to a minimum-security prison. It's a farm. They finally listened to him. They also talked to the guy he was arrested with. They offered to make him a deal if he told the truth about my brother. I think he's going to get out soon."

"You did the right thing," I said. It felt good to see her happy for a change.

"*You* did the right thing," she said.

Before I told the police about Alyssa, Dave Marsh had told them that I wanted them to promise that she would be protected. The cops agreed. They said that they would make sure it didn't look like she tipped them off because, well, she hadn't. I was glad she had decided to cooperate with them.

"So it all worked out," I said.

She hesitated.

"At first, I thought you were part of it," she said. "You know, because you were always there, cleaning up the evidence. And because you were always looking at me."

"That wasn't why I was looking at you," I said.

Her cheeks turned pink.

"So, now what?" she said. "I guess you're out of a job, huh?"

It was true. Ray's company had closed down.

"I have a job interview tomorrow," I said.

Dave Marsh had called me with the news. "You did a good thing, Colin," he said. "So, I got in touch with the utility company. They're still cleaning up graffiti. They want to offer you another job, if you're interested."

I said I was, and I thanked him.

"What about you?" I asked Alyssa.

"Same old, same old," she said. "Walking dogs, at least until my court date. They said I'd probably get probation and community service."

"It could be worse," I said.

"Yeah."

We looked at each other for a few moments.

"So I guess I'll see you around," I said finally.

She smiled again. It was as if the sun was coming out.

"I guess," she said.

Norah McClintock is the author of numerous mystery novels for kids and young adults, including *Bang, Tell* and *Snitch* in the Orca Soundings series. Norah lives in Toronto, Ontario.

Other Orca Currents titles:

121 Express Monique Polak

Camp Wild Pam Withers

Chat Room Kristin Butcher

Cracked Michele Martin Bossley

Crossbow Dayle Campbell Gaetz

Daredevil Club Pam Withers

Dog Walker Karen Spafford-Fitz

Finding Elmo Monique Polak

Flower Power Ann Walsh

Horse Power Ann Walsh

Hypnotized Don Trembath

Laggan Lard Butts Eric Walters

Manga Touch Jacqueline Pearce